Doesn't Fall Off His Horse

VIRGINIA A. STROUD

 BookPartners, LLC

For Grandpa Steve, who taught me
to see with clear eyes and an open heart
and to walk with a purpose

"Saygee"

Published by BookPartners, LLC
P.O.Box 790
Cedar Key, FL 32625-0790
(352) 543-9307
http://www.BookPartners.org

ISBN: 978-1-936495-00-9 (eBook)
ISBN: 978-1-936495-01-6 (Paperback)
ISBN: 978-1-936495-02-3 (Hardcover)

Designed by Telemachus Press, LLC
http://www.telemachuspress.com

Printed in the United States of America
10 9 8 7 6 5 4

Library of Congress Cataloging in Publication Data
Stroud, Virginia A.
Doesn't Fall Off His Horse / Virginia A. Stroud—1st ed.
p. cm.
Summary / Saygee's great-grandfather tells her the story of how he
got his name, Doesn't Fall Off His Horse.
ISBN 0-8037-1634-6 (trade)—ISBN 0-8037-1635-4 (lib. bdg.)
1. Kiowa Indians—Juvenile fiction. [1. Kiowa Indians—Fiction.
2. Indians of North America—Fiction. 3. Grandfathers—Fiction.] I. Title.
PZ7.S9248Do 1994 [E]—dc20 93-6271 CIP AC

The artwork was prepared with acrylic paint on Museum Rag paper.
It was then color-separated and reproduced in full color.

❖ Glossary ❖

coup (koo, from the French word for a sudden blow or strike): A sudden, successful act meant to dishonor an enemy.

coup stick: A willow stick, curved at the top and wrapped in otter skin; carried in battle by a warrior to tag the enemy.

hobble: A twisted rawhide rope tied around a horse's front legs to confine its movement.

lodge: A home or house.

lodge poles: Aspen poles used to support a tepee structure.

loo-loo: A high-pitched trill, produced with the tongue, made by the Plains Indian women to signify praise.

quiver: A case made of animal skin for holding arrows and a bow.

Saygee (Say-GEE, hard g as in good): An affectionate nickname among the Kiowa people meaning "youngest one" or "little one."

Tali (TAH-lee): Kiowa word for "boy."

tepee (TEE-pee): A large cone-shaped tent used as a dwelling place by the Plains Indians.

Saygee's great-grandfather was a slender man, and not very tall, but his hands and face showed his age, strength, and wisdom.

He sat on the edge of his bed facing the window, watching the patterns of light from the setting sun play on the fenced yard.
He watched the birds, the clouds, and a spider that was building its web. He watched the memories in his head.

"Grandpa," Saygee called softly. "Grandpa!"

This time he heard her. Slowly he turned his entire body around to face the doorway of his bedroom, his wire-framed glasses making his eyes look much larger than they really were.

A smile appeared across his face as he recognized his youngest great-granddaughter, and he raised his arm to greet Saygee. "Good to see you," he said. "Sit, sit." He slapped the bed beside him.

There were no exchanges of polite conversation with Grandpa, no "How are you, how have you been?" To him that was obvious: You were all right; you were with him.

They sat in silence as Saygee looked outdoors with him. When he was ready to talk, he would let her know.

In Saygee's household, children learned to watch for direction, not to ask questions; for the answers were available by watching. So she sat and watched with him for a bit, not wanting to interrupt his study of the earth. When his thoughts were finished, he patted her hand and smiled, giving her permission to speak.

Saygee wanted to ask Grandpa for a story, but which one? He was like a living book; nearly a hundred years had passed under his footsteps during his walk upon the earth. He had followed the buffalo, he had roamed the open plains with tepee and lodge poles, he'd seen the non-Indian wagons come to Indian Territory and watched from a hilltop as the settlers staked out the land. He saw one of the first locomotives cut across the prairie, then an automobile and an airplane; he had received the citizenship given to the Native American people. Many changes had come for his people, the Kiowas, in those years, and for him as well.

The little man's voice suddenly pierced the silence. "Doesn't Fall Off His Horse."

"Who doesn't fall off his horse, Grandpa?" Saygee asked.

"Me." He smiled with pride. "That's my Indian name, 'Doesn't Fall Off His Horse.'" He began to unfasten the top button of his red flannel shirt.

"You see?" He leaned forward. "See my neck—here, this side," and he motioned with the flat side of his left hand from his chin to his earlobe. "The bullet took half my neck. I thought I was a goner….But Doesn't Fall Off His Horse is still here, walking this good road," he added with a wink and a nod to Saygee.

Grandpa cleared his throat and reached for a cigarette off his nightstand. Saygee wrinkled her nose but remained quiet, listening.
"Over there," he said, pointing with his chin and lower lip. "Over there in that trunk is a white sheet. Bring it and its contents to me."

Saygee got up and headed toward the old leather-bound stagecoach trunk. Kneeling, she unfastened the wooden bar straps and opened the lid.

On top, just as Grandpa had said, was a long object wrapped in a white sheet. Grandpa reached out, impatient for her to lay the treasure in his lap. With one slow turn and another, he folded back the sheet. "There," he said, smiling as he exposed its contents.

"A quiver," Saygee said.

"Yes." He stroked the quiver gently. "Do you see the hide? It's leopard skin from India, very rare. I had to do a lot of trading with the white traders to get this hide. I exchanged one bow and two buffalo robes. It's my old friend. I took it everywhere with me—though there was a time when it didn't help me make a coup."

"What's a coup, Grandpa?" Saygee asked.

"Coup is like a game of tag—a very serious and dangerous game that we played to embarrass and show dishonor to the enemy tribes. A warrior could count coup in several ways. He could enter the enemy's village, run and touch a tepee with his bare hand, and leave without being caught; or in battle he might hit his enemy with an object in his hand—a bow, a lance, or a coup stick. The purpose was not to kill your enemy, but to shame him for being off guard. A

warrior counting coup could even steal horses from the enemy tribe."

"Steal horses, Grandpa?" Saygee interrupted, not believing her good grandpa would ever steal.

He smiled at her. "I know what you're thinking: It isn't right to steal. We would not have dreamed of taking a friend's possessions. But we sometimes took ponies from our enemies so they would be short of horses and could not raid our villages. This would also give our tribe fresh horses for our survival.

"Counting coup," Grandpa continued, "gave honor to the individual warrior and to the entire tribe. The warrior who made a coup was looked upon as a hero, and sometimes his warrior name would be earned.

"My friends and I would often hear the elder warriors speak of the coups they had made. We would sit, green with envy, listening spellbound to their adventures."

His eyes gazed out into the twilight sky. Then he began to speak again.

✣ ✣ ✣

"I don't know what year it was, because we didn't have calendars. It was a good time though.

"My friends and brothers were alive then, and active. We'd play

games with bows and arrows, perfecting our skills by hunting rabbits or even butterflies. We raced our ponies bareback in open fields, or watched the women make shields and tan the soft hides.

"To this day I have no idea which one of us began talking about stealing ponies from the Comanches camped south of us. But for days all we talked about were the ponies and the raid.

"I was sleeping on my pallet. Camp was silent. Then I heard a familiar voice outside my father's tepee whisper, 'Tonight, now, come.' It was my friend Tali, our ringleader.

"Getting out of our tepee without waking my parents would be much harder than raiding the Comanche ponies, I thought. I sat up, almost afraid to breathe. Mother was a light sleeper, and at any break in the breathing patterns of her children, she would rise quickly.

"I made my breath deep and even, so as not to cause alarm. Then I stood with my bow and leopard skin quiver in one hand, plotting my steps to the tepee flap across from me. I had to step around four bodies and get past the dogs to meet my friends. Part of me said, 'Just go'; the other part said, 'Lie back down!' One foot and then another and I was outside the tepee flap under open skies.

"'Come on, hurry!' whispered Tali, waving me over to join him and three others by the side of a tree. My steps were light as I ran in a crouched position, sweat beading over my lip and forehead.

"We were waiting for one more friend, but he had not yet appeared from his tepee. I felt a tap on my shoulder from behind and Tali beckoned me to follow. 'We can't wait any longer; it will be sunrise soon,' he said. 'As it is, we are going to have to ride hard to get to the Comanche camp without being seen!'

"Our ponies were hobbled in an area beside the stream. There was no moon, which made our escape easier. As we hid under the bellies of our ponies, we could see the watchers of the camp walking around the village. We threw blankets over the horses' heads so they wouldn't make any noise or rear up on us as we untied their hobbles and led them away from camp.

"A safe distance later we jumped on the ponies' backs, and away we rode toward the Comanche camp.

"My heart was pounding as we rode. I think the ponies sensed we were up to something; they were both fast and alert. Our goal was to enter the enemy camp, take their horses, and bring them back to our camp—all without being seen.

"The Oklahoma prairies were flat and full of prairie dog holes. The horses could step into the holes and break their legs, but we ran them as hard as we could all the same. When you're young, you sometimes do things that are not so smart. It's when you're older that you realize you should have taken precautions.

"As we rode farther south, the air carried the smell of smoke, and we knew we were close to the Comanche camp. Scrub oak bushes and cottonwood trees clustered by the stream.

"'We'll tie the ponies over there,' said Tali, pointing to the scrub oak. 'Reed will stay with our horses so they don't run off before we need them.'

"From here on we would approach on our stomachs, inching our way to the Comanche ponies tied across the campgrounds. 'Check the wind direction. Look for the camp watchers; nobody gives us away. If you get scared, stay put; don't stand or run.' These were our orders from Tali.

"I could still hear my heart pounding in my ears and quickly asked the Great Spirit to guide me; to help me gather my swiftness and intuition, and make my eyesight sharp and sense of smell keen as an animal's. 'Be as a deer,' I told myself.

"The Comanche ponies stirred as we approached. The watchers were nowhere in sight. We had to unhobble the horses, throw ropes around their necks, if time permitted, and escape. No time to use blankets to cover the eyes of the enemies' horses, so we grabbed their noses to keep them from making noises that would wake the village.

"I was hiding between the legs and bellies of the horses, working quickly to cut the hobbles. One kicked another in the flank; a fight was about to break out among them. I could see the whites of their eyes, and their ears were lying flat against their heads.

"'Let's go!' I heard. I grabbed the ropes that were around two of the horses' necks and mounted one of the Comanche ponies; my friends did the same. I herded the loose animals in front of me as we broke for open land.

"A man's deep voice called from behind our backs. We'd been spotted, and watchers were ready for us.

"A Comanche warrior jumped out from behind the scrub oak, startling my horse. The pony darted right, then left and around the man as he waved his raised arms above his head, warning me to stop.

I hung tightly to the lead ropes of the two horses that followed and continued to drive the loose ponies ahead of me.

"Ride hard. They are coming!" Reed shouted, pulling alongside us at full speed with our Kiowa ponies. I turned to see mounted Comanche warriors following close behind with rifles.

"Rifle fire zinged past my head, and I flattened myself against my horse's neck as its hooves pounded the prairie. I checked again behind me, and I could see the Comanche warriors slowing down.

As I sat upright on my horse, one more round of gunfire pierced the open skies.

"I felt warm liquid on my shoulder and face. Rain, I thought, and checked the starlit night sky. Then I sensed a burning sensation on my neck as my body recognized the wound.

"For a while everything seemed to move in slow-motion and the pounding hooves were silent. Still clutching the two horses' ropes,

I fell forward on my pony's neck, holding my arms and legs tight around its body. I had a sensation that someone was sitting behind me on the horse, sort of holding me in place, not letting me fall, as I bounced around like a rag doll.

"'Camp!' shouted Tali. 'Hold on!' The sun was breaking through the darkness. It wasn't over the horizon yet, but movement was visible in the camp. It was good to see the familiar clothes of my people.

"The women sang their high-pitched loo-loos of praise as they witnessed our approach. My friends whooped and yelled to celebrate our successful coup, awakening the rest of the village. My pony came to an abrupt halt, and I was carried off its back.

"Later I was told that my hands had to be pried from the ropes attached to the ponies that I'd pulled across the prairie. I had lost much blood, and half my neck was ripped loose from the Comanche bullet.

"The medicine woman housed me within the tepee walls of the medicine lodge. Her assistants cut a prickly leaf, split it, and placed it on my neck. No one thought I was going to live, but within four sunsets I was drinking water from a reed straw.

"When I was able to sit up on my own, four elders entered the medicine lodge together with family members and my friends from the raid.

"'What you boys did showed bad judgement,' said one of the elders.

"'You could have put this entire camp in danger with your foolishness,' said another. 'We are not at war with this enemy. Stealing horses is a war deed only!'

"'No one is permitted to make decisions on his own without the counsel of the tribal leaders,' the third one told me.

"'Also, what you did was very brave,' said the fourth elder. 'The people here needed fresh horses. For that you did well. You have been shot. That is enough punishment for you. Even though you were badly wounded, you didn't let go of your stolen horses or fall from your horse. You have made your first coup and have earned your warrior name. From now on you will be called "Doesn't Fall Off His Horse."' Then the elders left the medicine lodge.

"It took a long time to recover from my wounds, and that was the last time my friends and I raided alone."

Grandpa looked down at his leopard skin quiver and began to wrap the white sheet around it.

"I've never heard that story, Grandpa," Saygee said. "Today you found me remembering my youth, when my eyes were clear and my walk had purpose." He reached for his pillow, propped it behind him, and slowly leaned back on his bed, looking out the window and cradling his quiver. Then he took another cigarette, lit it, and said, "That's all."

Saygee knew that she was being dismissed. Her visit was over.

"Want your light on, Grandpa?" she asked. He didn't take his eyes away from the window, nor did he answer her. She could see that he was with his memories again; he was with Doesn't Fall Off His Horse.

CPSIA information can be obtained
at www.ICGtesting.com
Printed in the USA
LVIC04n1621070514
384803LV00015B/99